Mcc

Hey Diddle Diddle

and

Hey Diddle Doodle

Notes for adults

TADPOLES NURSERY RHYMES are structured to provide support for newly independent readers. The books may also be used by adults for sharing with young children.

The language of nursery rhymes is often already familiar to an emergent reader, so the opportunity to see these rhymes in print gives a highly supportive early reading experience. The alternative rhymes extend this reading experience further, and encourage children to play with language and try out their own rhymes.

If you are reading this book with a child, here are a few suggestions:

1. Make reading fun! Choose a time to read when you and the child are relaxed and have time to share the story.
2. Recite the nursery rhyme together before you start reading. What might the alternative rhyme be about? Why might the child like it?
3. Encourage the child to reread the rhyme, and to retell it in their own words, using the illustrations to remind them what has happened.
4. Point out together the rhyming words when the whole rhymes are repeated on pages 12 and 22 (developing phonological awareness will help with decoding language) and encourage the child to make up their own alternative rhymes.
5. Give praise! Remember that small mistakes need not always be corrected.

First published in 2008 by
Franklin Watts
338 Euston Road
London NW1 3BH

Franklin Watts Australia
Level 17/207 Kent Street
Sydney NSW 2000

Text (Hey Diddle Doodle)
© Brian Moses 2008
Illustration © Jill Newton 2008

The rights of Brian Moses to be identified as the author of Hey Diddle Doodle and Jill Newton as the illustrator of this Work have been asserted in accordance with the Copyright, Designs and Patents Act, 1988.

ISBN 978 0 7496 8031 2 (hbk)
ISBN 978 0 7496 8037 4 (pbk)

Series Editor: Jackie Hamley
Series Advisor: Dr Hilary Minns
Series Designer: Peter Scoulding

Printed in China

Franklin Watts is a division of
Hachette Children's Books
an Hachette Livre UK company.
www.hachettelivre.co.uk

Hey Diddle Diddle

Retold by Brian Moses
Illustrated by Jill Newton

W
FRANKLIN WATTS
LONDON•SYDNEY

**Jill
Newton**

"I live by the
sea in Somerset with
my dog, Bob, and my
horse, Spinney. I spend
my time running, riding
and drawing."

Hey diddle diddle,
the cat and the fiddle,

The cow jumped over the moon.

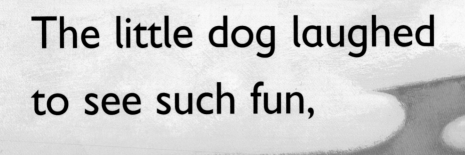

The little dog laughed
to see such fun,

9

And the dish ran away with the spoon!

11

Hey Diddle Diddle

Hey diddle diddle,

the cat and the fiddle,

The cow jumped over the moon.

The little dog laughed

to see such fun,

And the dish ran away

with the spoon!

Can you point to the
rhyming words?

Hey Diddle Doodle

by Brian Moses

Illustrated by Jill Newton

13

Brian Moses

"I have a golden labrador called Honey who spends a lot of her time trying to get through the garden fence to visit the poodle next door."

Hey diddle doodle,
the pipe and the poodle,

The frog hopped over the star.

The big tiger roared
to see such tricks,

18

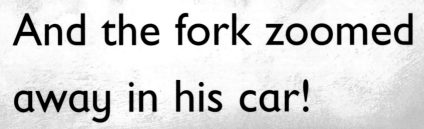

And the fork zoomed
away in his car!

Hey Diddle Doodle

Hey diddle doodle,

the pipe and the poodle,

The frog hopped over the star.

The big tiger roared

to see such tricks,

And the fork zoomed

away in his car!

Can you point to the
rhyming words?

Puzzle Time!

How many cats and dogs can you see in this picture?

Answers

There are 4 dogs,
and 6 cats.